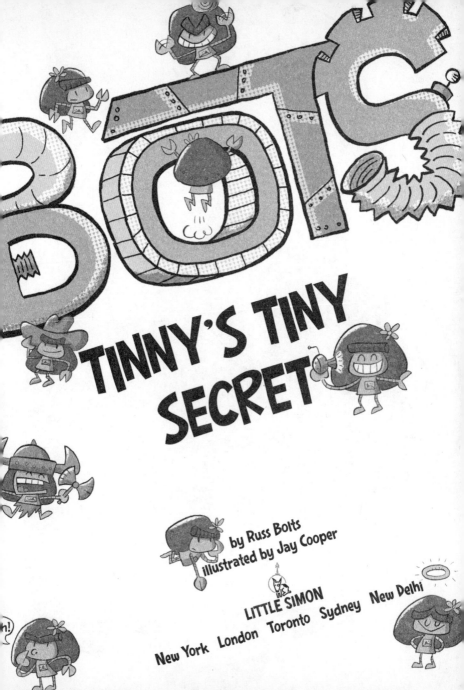

BOTS

TINNY'S TINY SECRET

by Russ Bolts
illustrated by Jay Cooper

LITTLE SIMON

New York London Toronto Sydney New Delhi

LITTLE SIMON
An imprint of Simon & Schuster Children's Publishing Division • 1230 Avenue of the Americas, New York, New York 10020 • First Little Simon hardcover edition November 2020 • Copyright © 2020 by Simon & Schuster, Inc. Also available in a Little Simon paperback edition. All rights reserved, including the right of reproduction in whole or in part in any form. LITTLE SIMON is a registered trademark of Simon & Schuster, Inc. and associated colophon is a trademark of Simon & Schuster, Inc. For information about special discounts for bulk purchases, please contact Simon & Schuster Special Sales at 1-866-506-1949 or business@simonandschuster.com. The Simon & Schuster Speakers Bureau can bring authors to your live event. For more information or to book an event contact the Simon & Schuster Speakers Bureau at 1-866-248-3049 or visit our website at www.simonspeakers.com. Manufactured in the United States of America 0920 FFG
2 4 6 8 10 9 7 5 3 1
Cataloging-in-Publication Data is available for this title from the Library of Congress.
ISBN 978-1-5344-7953-1 (hc)
ISBN 978-1-5344-7952-4 (pbk)
ISBN 978-1-5344-7954-8 (eBook)

CONTENTS

1

2

3

4

Oh, trust me. It's big.

What is a Big Blooper anyway?

You don't know?

Um, uh, well, of course I know, but for the fans out there who don't know what the Big Blooper is, you should tell them.

6

9

19

Unfortunately, not everyone loved school that day.

20

21

22

Ah, the students are in class now.

With all the Big Bloopers put away, there should not be any surprises.

28

CHAPTER 3

Blame Game

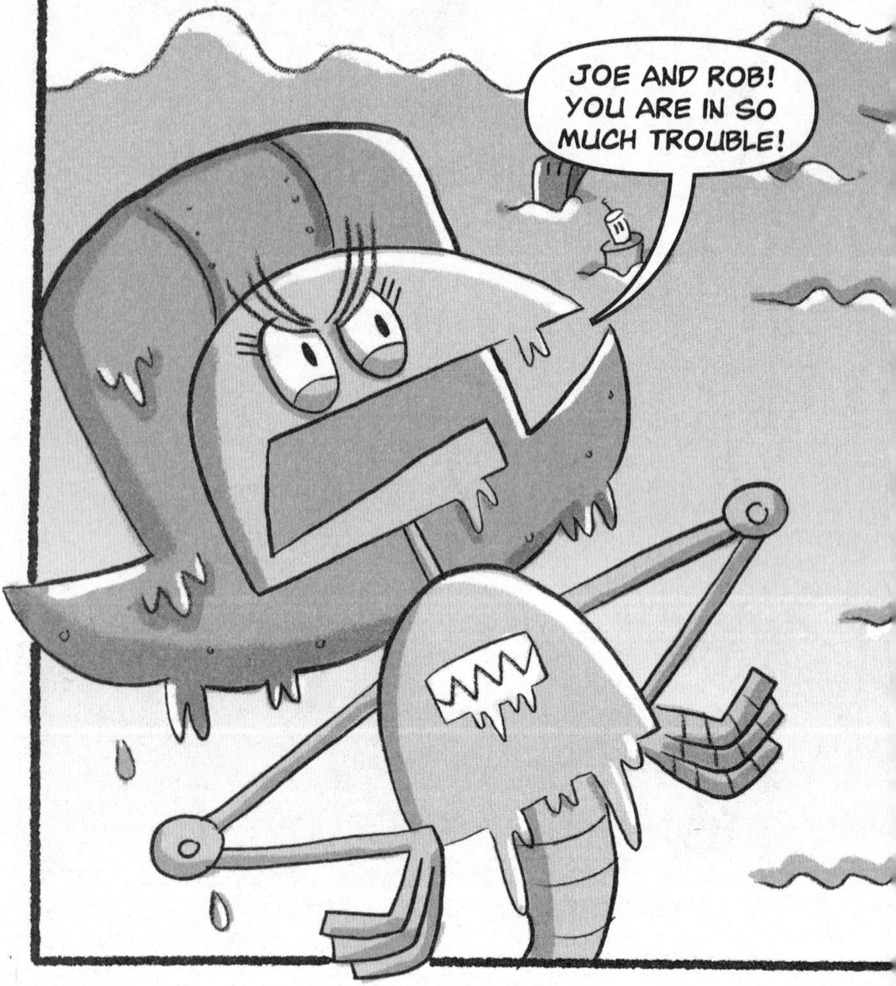

34

CHAPTER 4
The Principal's Office

Oh dear. The Principal's office... wait, is that bad?

Popular visitors

Principal's Office

Abandon All Hope, Ye Who Enter Here.

WRONG PENCILS!

Certainly some good kids are sent to the Principal's office for awards or prizes for being so good.

39

We call your parents.

We call your grandparents.

Detention.

Gym detention.

A mark on your permanent record.

Must wear the Hat of Shame...forever!

44

45

ET GO.

47

48

49

51

CHAPTER 5

Tinny Trouble

Meanwhile, back in class, Tinny was very happy.

57

59

61

CHAPTER 6

A Tiny Secret

And so Tinny took off through the halls in search of Joe and Rob.

64

75

79

To save Joe and Rob, I have to think like Joe and Rob.

Duh, I am Joe, and I like to fart.

Duh, I am Rob, and I like Joe's farts.

I've got a plan so dumb, it just might work.

86

89

Cracking Up

FREEDOM

99

This way!

THEY ARE NOT IN HERE.

CHAPTER 10

Trophy Time

In case you were worried about the school, don't. Tinny's plan worked, and all the students were very excited.

119

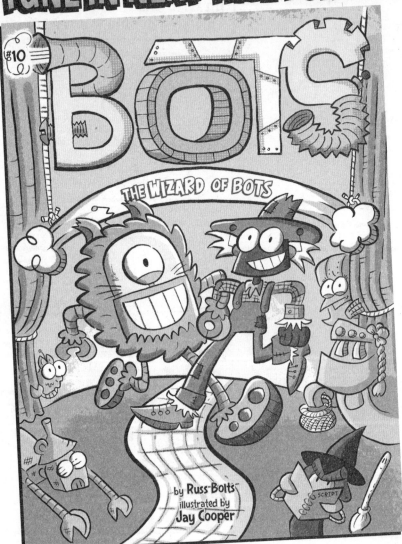

TUNE IN NEXT TIME FOR...

#10

BOTS

THE WIZARD OF BOTS

by Russ Bolts
illustrated by
Jay Cooper

SCRIPT